Borgon the Axeboy

AND THE
PRINCE'S
SHADOW

ALSO IN THIS SERIES

Borgon the Axeboy and the Dangerous Breakfast

ABOUT THE AUTHOR

KJARTAN POSKITT is the well-loved author of many hilarious books for children including Agatha Parrot and the Murderous Maths series, translated into over 30 languages. With a background in children's television, he is a tireless and brilliant performer.

ABOUT THE ILLUSTRATOR

PHILIP REEVE is an award-winning illustrator and author whose books have won the Carnegie, Guardian and Smarties Prizes.

Borgon the Axeboy

the Axeboy

AND THE
PRINCE'S
SHADOW

Kjartan
Poskitt

Illustrated by
Philip
Reeve

ff

FABER & FABER

First published in 2015
by Faber & Faber Limited
Bloomsbury House
74–77 Great Russell Street
London WC1B 3DA

Designed by Faber
Printed and bound by CPI Group (UK) Ltd, Croydon CR4 0YY

A CIP record for this book is available from the British Library

978–0571–30735–7

FSC
www.fsc.org
MIX
Paper from
responsible sources
FSC® C101712

2 4 6 8 10 9 7 5 3 1

To Harry and Max

Meet the savages!

BORGON,

our hero!

GRIZZY,

Borgon's annoying

next-cave neighbour

FULGUT,
Borgon's dad

FULMA,
Borgon's mum

MUNGOID and HUNJAH, Borgon's pals

GOLGARTH BASIN

THE
FIRE LANDS

RARGH!

HERE BE DRAGONS

THE PUNCH PIT

THE UPSIDE-DOWN
MOUNTAINS

THE
LOST DESERT

MOUNTAINS OF CHAOS

BOO-BA-DE-DOO

WAH OOOH

SHABBADA BE-BOO-BA DOOP

YEAH!

VALLEY OF THE SCAT CACTI

THE WANDERING JUNGLE

CONFUSED BUSH

THE LOST DESSERT

N

RUINED TEMPLE

The Vultures' Surprise

TUB-ARP TUB-ARP!

It was early morning in the Lost Desert, and high up in the yellow sky, two ragged vultures were looking down to see what was making all the noise. They were hovering above a wide stone plain known as Golgarth Stretch. A wooden stage had been set up in the middle and standing on it was a fat blue slave with a two-headed trumpet. He gave it another mighty blast . . .

TUB-ARP TUB-ARP!

The sound echoed across the desert and slipped into the cave where Borgon the Axeboy was having his breakfast. Borgon was a barbarian, so he always ate his breakfast the barbarian way. This

meant chopping lumps from a fat elephant tongue with his axe, and shoving them into his mouth as quickly and as messily and as noisily as he could.

CHOP CHOMP SLURP!
CHOP CHOMP SLURP!

The elephant tongue was exactly how Borgon liked them. It was burnt on the outside and juicy in the middle, but most importantly it was a BIG elephant tongue. If Borgon was going to eat something, he didn't really care how hot it was or even how dead it was, just so long as it was big.

TUB-ARP TUB-ARP! came the noise again.

Borgon's mum came hurrying out from the back of the cave. Fulma was a tall slim savage with long fingers, mad spiky hair and dark narrow eyes.

'Did you hear that?' she asked. 'I wonder what it is?'

'Whatever it is, it's very bad manners,' said Borgon, doing a **BURP**. 'I can hardly hear myself eat.'

TUB-ARP TUB-ARP!

Borgon's dad came out of the back of the cave to join them. Fulgut was a very big sleepy old savage.

'I know that noise,' he said. 'It's the fanfare for the Shadow Trials.'

'The what?' asked Borgon.

'It's a competition that the palace organise,' explained Fulgut. 'They do it whenever they need a new bodyguard for the prince. The winner has to stay with him day and night, so they call him the Prince's Shadow.'

'Why does the prince need a bodyguard?' asked Borgon. 'The whole palace is built like a castle. Nobody can get inside.'

'That's not the problem!' chuckled Fulma. 'The danger's already there.'

'I thought the palace people were all harmless,' said Borgon. 'You told me they just lie around all day inventing laws that everybody ignores.'

'Yes, but some of them can't be trusted,' said Fulma. 'They'll be nice to you in the daytime, but then they'll murder you in your sleep.'

'What, without having a good fight first?' said Borgon. 'That's cheating!'

'Dead right,' said Fulgut. 'But that's what posh people are like. All cheats and liars.'

'Why don't they get one of the palace guards to be the Shadow?' asked Borgon.

'Are you kidding?' said Fulgut. 'They're too soft and lazy. The palace need a savage for the job.'

'Then you should have a go, Dad,' said Borgon.

'Me?' laughed Fulgut. 'We're barbarians, son. We're far too rough and smelly for the palace. They'd never want the likes of us in there.'

'That's their problem, not ours,' said
Borgon. 'If they want the best bodyguard,
then that's you. You've always been the
fiercest, toughest and scariest savage in the
desert. Come on, Dad, where's your pride?
Get out there and show them what a real
barbarian can do!'

'They won't be interested,' said Fulgut.
'The only savages the palace like are those
flashy Raggahoos.'

'The Raggahoos are hardly savages,'
giggled Fulma. 'They use soap!'

'Soap?' asked Borgon.
'What's that?'

'It's something you rub

on your skin,' said Fulma. 'It's like having a
flower be sick on you.'

'YUK!' said Borgon. 'That settles it. Dad,
you're going to compete in the trials, and
you're going to win.'

'I'm too busy,'
said Fulgut, with
a big lazy yawn.
'It's turned a
bit chilly this
morning. I need
to find my thick
socks.'
'Thick socks?'
moaned Borgon.

'Dad, you're a BARBARIAN! You should
be fighting six-headed bulls, you should
be walking through fire, you should be
attacking whole armies on your own. You
should NEVER be looking for a pair of thick
socks. Tell him, Mum!'

But Fulma was staring in the cracked
old mirror hanging on their wall. She was
pulling a bone comb through her hair,

which suddenly
snapped. Her mad
hair immediately
knotted itself up to
look like an old
bird's nest.

'Oh rattlesnakes!' she sighed. 'That was my last good comb. I'll never control my hair now.'

'Mum!' wailed Borgon. 'You're a barbarian too, so your hair doesn't matter. Tell her, Dad!'

'They're blue,' said Fulgut, still looking for his socks. 'You know the ones I mean? I knitted them myself.'

Borgon almost choked. It was bad enough that his mum was worried about her hair, and now his dad was knitting his own socks! It was a really depressing start to the day. And it was just about to get worse.

'Hello!' came a voice from the cave entrance. 'Can I come in?'

'No!' said Borgon.

'But it's your friend Grizzy,' said Fulma.

'She's NOT my friend,' said Borgon.

Grizzy was a savage girl who lived in one of the other caves nearby. She had a bad habit of skipping and being irritating and generally sticking her nose in where it wasn't wanted. And Borgon definitely didn't want her nose sticking into his breakfast. He might accidentally chop it off and chomp it, and then she'd moan at him for EVER.

'Hey, Borgon,' said Grizzy excitedly. 'Are you going to watch the Shadow Trials? If you are, can I come too?'

'No I'm not,' said Borgon. 'So no you can't. Goodbye.'

'Aw!' said Grizzy, sounding disappointed. 'But look here . . .'

She reached into her bag and pulled out the little book she always carried. It was called the *Book of All Things*. The three barbarians watched as she flicked through to find the right page. None of them could read, so they had no idea how the strange little flappy thing could put words in Grizzy's head. In fact, they thought it was all a bit spooky. Oo-er!

'The Shadow Trials,' read Grizzy. 'Contestants will face extreme challenges of endurance, speed and courage.' She shut the book and looked at Borgon. 'I can't believe you're not going.'

'He doesn't have to go if he doesn't want to,' said Fulma. 'It'll just be a lot of silly people with swords and blood and fighting and screaming and dying.'

'WHAT?' said Borgon. He immediately tucked his axe into one side of his belt, and the rest of the elephant tongue into the other side for later. 'That sounds brilliant.

Come on, everybody, let's go!'

By now Fulgut had found one big blue sock, but was still looking for the other one.

'Not me,' said the big old savage. 'I've got a sock to find.'

'How about you, Mum?' asked Borgon.

'Me?' said Fulma. 'I can't go out with my hair like this!'

'Honestly!' said Borgon crossly. 'Call yourselves barbarians? You two are USELESS and EMBARRASSING. I'll just have to go on my own, then.'

Borgon stomped off out of the cave.

'Wait for me!' said Grizzy, running after him.

'I'm going on my own!'

'But with me coming too,' said Grizzy.

'No, I'm going all alone, by myself.'

'I know,' said Grizzy. 'And you will be all alone, by yourself, but with me.'

'ON MY VERY OWN.'

'With me.'

And so it was that Borgon the Axeboy went marching out towards the stone plains of Golgarth Stretch all alone, on his very own, by himself.

With Grizzy.

The Savage with Zebra Legs

The last few people were making their way across Golgarth Stretch to join the crowd around the stage. Borgon was walking with them, trying to ignore Grizzy skipping alongside him. She'd been talking the whole way.

'It's exciting, isn't it?' she said.

'I can't wait, can you?' she said.

'Not far to go now, is it?' she said.

Suddenly Borgon stopped dead in his tracks.

'That's it,' said Borgon. 'One more word from you and I'm going home.'

'OK,' said Grizzy. But then she realised she'd said one more word. 'Sorry,' she said. 'I didn't mean to say that. And I didn't mean to say that either. Or that. Or that. Or that.'

Borgon glared at her.

'Not ONE MORE word,' he said.

Grizzy clamped her hands over her mouth to show she was trying her best, but then she saw something charging up behind them.

'Mm mm mmmm mm!' said Grizzy, pointing back across the Stretch.

'Forget it,' said Borgon, sticking his fingers in his ears. 'I'm not listening.'

'Mm mm mmmm mm!' said Grizzy, her eyes wide open in alarm.

'Can't hear you,' said Borgon, jamming his fingers in even more tightly.

'Mm mm mmmm mm!' said Grizzy, jumping up and down.

Borgon still couldn't hear Grizzy, so she grabbed him and pulled him aside just as a huge horse shot past right where he'd been standing.

'OUT OF MY WAY!' shouted the rider. He was a tall savage wearing shiny, zebra-skin trousers. The horse was still charging forwards and heading straight at two boys. One was skinny and wearing a straw hat, the other was as chunky as a pile of bricks.

'Oh no,' said Borgon. 'It's Hunjah and Mungoid!'

Borgon's two friends tried to dive clear, but

then Hunjah's hat fell off. He stopped to pick
it up, but just as the horse was about to hit
him, Mungoid stepped in the way.

SCREEEE . . . KRUMP!

The horse hit Mungoid full-on, then staggered backwards and came to a stop with Zebra Legs desperately struggling to stay on its back. The chunky savage wobbled slightly, but stayed on his feet.

Borgon and Grizzy ran up to see what was happening.

'Why aren't you dead?' Zebra Legs shouted at Mungoid.

'Sorry, mate,' said Mungoid. 'I just didn't fancy it.'

'He's a special sort of savage,' explained Hunjah. 'He's a stone-eater. He's as solid and as heavy as a rock.'

'Then why did he step in front of my

horse? He could have killed it!'

'So what?' said Hunjah. 'You could have squashed my hat.'

'Are you two trying to make me look stupid?' demanded Zebra Legs.

'We don't need to,' said Hunjah.

'You're the one riding your horse like an idiot,' said Mungoid.

'You'll be sorry you said that!' cried Zebra Legs. With a flash, he whipped out his sword from his belt, but then Borgon went and stood in front of them.

'Oi, Mr Fancy Trousers!' shouted Borgon. 'What kind of coward are you? You can see those two haven't got weapons.'

'I'm not scared of weapons,' said Zebra Legs.

'Oh no?' said Borgon. He reached down to grab his axe from his belt. 'You should be scared of this one!'

Zebra Legs gave Borgon a funny look. Then everybody gave Borgon a funny look. Even the horse gave Borgon a funny look.

Borgon couldn't understand it. He was a BARBARIAN! And there was nothing more frightening than a barbarian waving his axe.

'**GRRRR!**' growled Borgon, just to remind everybody how frightening he was.

To Borgon's amazement, Zebra Legs just smiled.

'**GRRRR!**' growled Borgon again.

'Ha ha ha!' laughed the savage.

'Borgon . . .' said Mungoid.

'Not now, Mungoid' said Borgon. 'I'm busy saying **GRRRR!**'

'Yes I know,' said Mungoid. 'But it would be better if you were holding your axe.'

'I AM holding my . . .'

Then Borgon looked at his hand. It turned out that Borgon had only *thought* he'd pulled his axe from his belt.

Unfortunately when he'd gone to grab it he'd made a mistake, and instead of his axe he'd been waving the squelchy end of the elephant tongue.

'It's a good job *you're* not competing in the Shadow Trials,' laughed Zebra Legs. 'You'd be dead in no time!'

And with that, the zebra-legged savage galloped on towards the stage.

Borgon growled. He was thinking of something nasty and frightening to shout, but then a strange smell drifted up his nose.

SNIFF SNIFF went Borgon.

SNIFF SNIFF went the others.

SNIFF they all went together.

'This might sound silly,' said Mungoid.
'But can anybody else smell something like
. . . flower sick?'

Cheers, Boos and Ragga Ragga Hoo Hoos!

Borgon and the others joined the back of the crowd, just as the fat blue slave held up his trumpet again. He did one final, and very important sounding, **TUB-ARRPPP!**

A very elegant lady slowly stepped up on to the stage. She wore a striped top hat and she had a long pointed nose. She was using a tall staff to lean on, which had a large silver crystal on the top.

'Wow!' said Grizzy excitedly. 'That's Dame Madreesh!'

'Who?' asked the others.

'She's one of the most important people in the palace,' said Grizzy. 'They say she's as old as the mountains.'

Everyone went quiet as the dame inspected the crowd. There were people of all different sizes and colours. There were big people, skinny people, bald people, spiky-haired people, people wearing thick metal armour, people wearing nothing, and nearly everybody was carrying some

sort of nasty weapon.

'Welcome, savages!' said Madreesh. Her voice was a strong low purr, like a lion snoring.

'**YARGHHHHH!**' cheered the crowd, waving their weapons in the air.

'I come from the palace to seek the prince's new Shadow,' said the dame. 'Contenders, present yourselves!'

TUB-ARP! went the trumpet. Three savages climbed up the steps and stood in a line along the stage. There was a fat one, a bony one and one with curly hair. They were all wearing zebra-skin tunics and each one had a sword. Suddenly a fourth savage leapt

up on to the stage behind

them and pushed his way to

the front. It was Zebra Legs

himself.

'I am Akabbah the champion!' he

shouted to the crowd. Then, for no

reason at all, he jumped up and did a neat

backflip before landing perfectly on his

feet again.

'Oooooh!' went the crowd and everybody gave him a cheer.

All four savages on the stage started to chant:

RAGGA RAGGA HOO HOO!
RAGGA RAGGA HOO HOO!

'I might have guessed,' said Borgon. 'That's the Raggahoo tribe. Dad says that one of them always wins these trials.'

'It's obvious which one it's going to be too,' said Mungoid.

Akabbah was swaggering around at the front of the stage while the others looked a bit grumpy.

Madreesh spoke to the four Raggahoos.

'Contenders, prepare to face the three Shadow Trials. The first trial is a test of endurance and the second is a test of speed. The final trial is the terrible test of courage.'

There were disappointed murmurs from the crowd.

'What about a COMBAT trial?' shouted a big woman with an eyepatch. 'We want them to fight to death!'

'DEATH DEATH DEATH!' cheered the crowd.

The four Raggahoos on stage glanced at each other nervously.

'The trials do not require savages to kill

each other,' said Madreesh.

'How about if they hurt
each other a lot?' shouted
a huge man with rusty
metal teeth.

'HURT A LOT,
HURT A LOT, HURT
A LOT!' cheered the crowd.

The old dame shook her head.

'Suppose they just make each other slightly
sore?' shouted a skinny man with iron spikes
coming out of his head.

'SLIGHLY SORE, SLIGHTLY SORE,
SLIGHTLY SORE!' cheered the crowd.

The four Raggahoos were still looking

uneasy. Akabbah went up to Madreesh.

'I thought you were supposed to be
in charge,' he said. 'So get this
lot sorted out, you silly old
woman.'

The dame's long nose
twitched crossly.

'Don't worry, little boy,' she
said. 'There is NO official combat trial . . .'

'Booo!' went the crowd.

'. . . unless two of you challenge each
other.'

Everybody looked at the contestants. The
four Raggahoos had relaxed again, and were
strutting about trying to look tough, and

doing dainty little swipes with their swords.
The crowd groaned. There wasn't much
chance of seeing two of them wanting to
fight to the death.

'What a waste of time,' said Mungoid.
'I don't want to watch this.'

'I think I'd rather clean my hat,' said
Hunjah.

'I think I'd rather watch you clean your
hat,' said Mungoid.

'You're right,' said Borgon. 'This is boring.
I'll see you all later.'

'But we only just got here!' said Grizzy.
'Don't go home now.'

'Who said anything about going home?'

said Borgon. 'I'm just going to liven things up a bit.'

Borgon pushed past the blue slaves guarding the steps. Before they could stop him, he was up on the stage.

'Excuse me!' he called out towards the Raggahoos.

'Oh look!' said Akabbah. 'It's the little fat boy with the smelly meat.'

A few people in the crowd laughed.

'Get him off here!' said Akabbah.

Two of the big blue slaves came to drag Borgon away, but Madreesh waved them back. She stood aside and watched as Borgon walked over to the tall savage with the

zebra-skin trousers.

'I've got something for you,' said Borgon.

Akabbah and the others all drew their swords.

'Go away,' he said. 'Go on, before you get killed.'

'I told you before,' said Borgon. 'You can't kill me while I'm holding this!'

He pulled the elephant tongue from his belt. It was still wet and nicely sticky.

'I'll kill you if I want to!' shouted Akabbah.

The tall savage lunged forward, but . . .

SHPLOPP!

. . . Borgon had already thrown the tongue.

It hit Akabbah right in the face and stuck there. As the tall savage scraped the mess out of his eyes, Borgon caught the end of the sword in the curve of his axe blade. He gave it a sharp twist, the sword pinged free and Akabbah fell backwards.

Akabbah leapt up to attack again, then saw that the end of his sword was curled up. He tried to stab it into Borgon's stomach, but it just rolled up even more and made a little **DOY YOY YOING!** noise.

'Ha ha ha!' laughed the crowd. Even the other three Raggahoos at the back of the stage had their hands over their mouths, trying to hide the giggles.

Borgon tucked his axe back into his belt.

'Job done,' he said.

Borgon turned to leave the stage but the dame stopped him.

'Going already?' she said. 'I thought you were a contestant.'

'Do I look like one of them?' asked Borgon, pointing at the four Raggahoos in their zebra skins.

'No, but the trials are open to any savage,' said Madreesh.

'Have a go!' shouted Eyepatch Woman.

'Yeah, get stuck in there!' called out Mr Rusty Teeth.

'The more the merrier!' shouted Spike-Head Man.

The whole crowd began to cheer, but Borgon wasn't interested.

'No thanks,' he said to the dame. 'I thought there would be loads of tough savages doing these trials, but I can't be bothered to take on this bunch of damp-panted dandies.'

'Ha ha ha!' laughed the crowd.

Akabbah jumped in front of Borgon.

'Hold it right there,' he said. 'If you think

these trials are so soft, why don't you have a go?'

'Because I'm going to watch my friend clean his hat,' said Borgon. 'It'll be far more exciting than anything you lot can do.'

He pushed past the lanky savage.

'Very funny,' said Akabbah. 'Because I say you're scared.'

Borgon stopped.

'Scared?' he repeated. 'I'm a BARBARIAN. I'm not scared of anything.'

'Oh no?' said Akabbah. 'Then let's sort this out once and for all. I challenge you to a combat trial! Right here and right now.'

One of the other Raggahoos tossed

Akabbah a new sword. In a flash, Borgon's
axe was back in his hand.

'Watch your back, Borgon!' shouted
Mungoid from the crowd.

Sure enough, the other three Raggahoos
were also pointing their swords at Borgon.

'Bring them ON!' shouted Borgon.

'Hooray!' cheered the crowd.

'STOP!' commanded the dame. 'We
are looking for a champion, not a dead
body.'

'You're going to get FOUR dead bodies,'
said Borgon. **'YARGHHHH!'**

He charged across the stage waving his
axe. The Raggahoos all leapt backwards in

terror, but the dame flicked out the end of
her staff and caught Borgon round the ankle.
He fell flat on his face.

WHEEE BLAM!

'Ha ha ha!' laughed everyone.

TUB–ARP! went the blue slave.

Of course Borgon wasn't laughing, but neither were the Raggahoos. The tall savages all looked a bit shocked.

'Tell me, barbarian,' said the dame. 'What is your name?'

Borgon was too cross to answer, so Mungoid answered for him.

'He's Borgon the Axeboy,' he shouted.

'Borgon!' smiled the dame. 'Would you like to take part in the trials?'

'Oh go on, Borgon!' shouted Mungoid. 'Do it!'

'Yeah, go on!' said Hunjah. 'I can always clean my hat later.'

Borgon shook his head.

'Are you sure?' asked Madreesh. 'Everyone here would really appreciate it.'

A big cheer went up from the crowd.

'Everyone?' said Borgon.

The dame looked over to where the four Raggahoos were skulking at the far end of the stage. The corner of her mouth curved into a sneaky smile. 'Well, there are four people who'd rather you didn't,' she admitted.

Borgon grinned.

'Then I'll do it!' he said.

The Mountains of Chaos

The vultures were still hovering high up
above the stage. They had been watching
everything with great interest, especially
when Borgon had got his axe out. The
vultures weren't silly. With a bit of luck
there would soon be something on the
stage for them to eat!

Down in the crowd, Grizzy was reading her *Book of All Things*.

'Borgon's going to make a real fool of himself,' said Grizzy. 'He won't even pass the first trial.'

'Why not?' asked Mungoid.

'It's a sort of race,' said Grizzy. 'How is little fat Borgon going to keep up with that lot?'

'Simple,' said Mungoid. 'Borgon's a barbarian. If he can't do something the right way, he'll do it the wrong way.'

'I still can't see how Borgon will get through this,' said Grizzy, checking her book. 'First they send a Bigfoot slave up the mountains. He lays out a trail of blue stones, and he leaves some giant rubies at the top. Once he's got back, the challengers have to race up to collect a ruby each to show they've been there. The last one back loses.'

'Why do they send a Bigfoot?' asked Hunjah.

'Because the Bigfoots know their way around,' said Grizzy. 'And those are the Mountains of Chaos. A lot of people go there and never find their way back again.'

'So they die?' said Hunjah.

'Of course,' said Grizzy. 'And if you die you're not allowed to do the next trial. That's the rules.'

'Look!' said Mungoid. 'There's the Bigfoot coming back now. They'll soon be off.'

Sure enough a tall hairy savage was sprinting back from the mountains, dropping blue stones along the way.

Up on the

stage, Borgon had picked up the
elephant tongue and was giving it a
good chew. Akabbah had gathered
the other three Raggahoos together
in the corner and was whispering
to them.

'Hey, Borgon!' shouted
Mungoid. 'You be careful.
That lot are up to something.'

'Thank goodness!' grinned
Borgon. 'It would be boring if they
weren't.'

TUB-ARP went the trumpet.

'Contenders, prepare!' ordered
the dame.

Borgon and the Raggahoos lined up at the edge of the stage, ready to leap off and run to the mountains.

TUB-ARP went the trumpet again.

'GO!' shouted everybody.

So they went.

Borgon and the Raggahoos raced along the trail of blue stones. Akabbah was in front, but Borgon was keeping right on his heels. The chubby little barbarian was faster than he looked.

'Give up now,' said Akabbah. 'You'll never make it to the top!'

'Why not?' puffed Borgon. 'I'm as fit as any of you.'

'Ha!' laughed Akabbah. 'Do you really think we're going to let you get there?'

They followed the trail as it twisted and turned up the mountain slope between a set of giant boulders. As soon as they were out of sight of the stage, Akabbah spun round and caught Borgon with a surprise flying kick. Borgon fell over, and before he could get up, the other three had pounced on him and pinned him down.

'You just stay there like a good boy,' laughed Akabbah.

The tall savage dashed ahead, leaving the others sitting on Borgon.

'YARGHHHH!' cried Borgon. He twisted

and kicked, and finally managed to throw them off. He leapt up, waving his axe. The three savages quickly retreated back down the path.

'If you want a fight, then get your swords out,' said Borgon. 'But be quick, because I've got a ruby to collect.'

The three savages shook their heads nervously.

'Please yourselves,' said Borgon, then he left them and ran off up the mountain.

The blue stones took him zigzagging in and out of rock stacks, ducking under arches, scrambling up slopes and then down into a long dark tunnel. Borgon was just

coming out the other end when he tripped
on something and fell with a clatter.

It was a skeleton, still wearing a faded
green dress and a big sun hat and clutching
an empty picnic bag. Oh dear. Some poor

lady had obviously thought the mountains were a nice place to wander round and have a spot of lunch. But there had been too much wandering and not enough lunch.

Borgon got back on his feet, and ran out of the tunnel. He found himself making his way along a ledge. On one side was a steep rock wall, on the other was a deep dark crack in the ground. The ledge was getting narrower and narrower and then . . .

KURR-EEEEK!

Borgon looked up to see a zebra-trousered leg kick a heavy stone slab down towards him. There was no time to get away. All Borgon could do was swing his axe upwards as hard as he could.

KADDA-RACK!

The axe smashed
the slab into dust.
Borgon pushed
himself against
the wall, so he
was out of
sight from
above, then
cried out as
if he were
falling into
the deep
dark crack.

'ARGHHHHHHHHH!'

'Ha ha ha!' came Akabbah's voice from above. 'Goodbye for ever, chubby boy.'

Borgon heard Akabbah run off, then he smiled to himself. If Akabbah thought he was dead, he wouldn't try to ambush him again. Good.

Borgon followed the trail until he saw Akabbah in the distance, jogging up to the top of a rocky peak. Akabbah stopped beside an old tree stump, then he picked something off the top of it. He tucked it into his shirt, then raised his face towards the sky.

'RAGGA RAGGA HOO HOO!'

he cheered triumphantly.

'RAGGA RAGGA HOO HOO!'

The sound echoed around the rocks from all sides. From somewhere in the distance far below came three voices in reply:

RAGGA RAGGA HOO HOO!

Akabbah had told the others he'd reached the end of the trail.

Those zebra legs were already running back down the path, so Borgon needed to hide. Unfortunately there was no little cave to slip into or rock stack to duck behind. Borgon had to think quickly – where could he go?

PUDDOB! PUDDOB! PUDDOB!

Akabbah's footsteps thudded along the

narrow ledge, then they went into the tunnel and passed the skeleton in the faded green dress and big sun hat.

PUDDOB! PUDDOB! PUDDOB!

The footsteps ran off into the distance.

It's a shame Akabbah didn't look back. He would have seen the skeleton take her hat off and slip out of her dress.

ARGHH!

But actually it was only Borgon who neatly dressed the skeleton again and gave her back her picnic bag.

'Thanks,' he said.

Borgon left his new friend in the tunnel and made his way up to the rocky peak.

There was no sign of the other three Raggahoos coming, but surely they couldn't be far behind him by now?

When Borgon got to the old tree stump, all he could see was an empty bird's nest. He picked up the nest, looked underneath, turned it over and shook it, but there were no rubies inside.

'Oh rattlesnakes!' cursed Borgon.

Suddenly it was obvious what the Raggahoos had planned. Akabbah had taken all the rubies! No wonder the others hadn't bothered to keep up with him. The four of them would go back with a ruby each and pretend they'd all been up the mountain. Borgon wouldn't have one and there was nothing he could do about it.

The Yellow Egg

Borgon sat down on the tree stump and thought hard. Somehow he had to prove that he had reached the end of the trail, and the other three Raggahoos had not. He needed something to show the dame, but there was only the bird's nest, a few stones and a dead scorpion, and they wouldn't prove anything!

Borgon kicked the tree stump in frustration.

KRUMPP!

Something rolled out from
a hole in the bottom of the
stump. It was a bright yellow
egg. It must have fallen out of the
nest when the Bigfoot had put the
rubies in, or when Akabbah had
taken them out. Either way, it was such a
strange-looking thing, the Bigfoot would be
sure to remember it!

Borgon picked up the egg, then made his
way back to the skeleton in the tunnel. He
borrowed the picnic bag and put the egg
inside to keep it safe, then set off again,

following the trail of blue stones. All around him was a jumble of rocky slopes, arches and boulders.

'No wonder these are called the Mountains of Chaos!' he said to himself.

In the distance, Borgon heard a triumphant cheer.

RAGGA RAGGA HOO HOO!

Obviously Akabbah had met up with the other Raggahoos and they were feeling very pleased with themselves.

'You've made a big mistake, lads,' muttered Borgon. 'There's nothing clever about trying to cheat a barbarian!'

Borgon followed the trail round a few

boulders, under an arch and then stopped. The blue stones had come to an end. He ran ahead and stuck his head round a corner. No good. He came back and tried setting off in different directions. There were no more blue stones, just the ones leading back to the tree stump.

That sneaky zebra-legged freak! thought Borgon. *He collected up the blue stones, just in case I survived!*

Borgon dropped to his knees to see if there were any tracks he could follow. A footprint in the dust, a tiny scratch on a rock, even a few overturned pebbles would give him a clue. There was nothing.

The sun was getting hotter, and the rocks around him were starting to glow. Borgon thought of the poor woman in the tunnel. He didn't want to end up like her! He HAD to find a way back.

Just then he felt something moving in the bag. He looked inside and saw that the eggshell was broken. At first Borgon thought he must have cracked it, but when he reached in to see, something nipped at his finger. He opened the bag right up. A little face was staring at him.

'Quammy,' it said.

It was a little yellow sand duck.

'Quammy?' it said again.

'Do you mean mummy?' asked Borgon.
'I'm not your mummy!'

The little duck stuck her head out of the
bag, then spotted something in the distant sky.

'Quammy!' she said. 'Quammy quammy
quammy!'

Borgon saw the duck was staring at two
ragged dots.

'Quammy,' said the duck.

'Your mummy isn't one of those.' said
Borgon. 'Those are just the vultures over the
stage . . . Oh!'

Suddenly Borgon knew which way to go,

and it was all thanks to the baby duck! He made his way towards the two dots, leaping over rocks and scrambling down ledges. It wasn't long before he heard voices calling:

'Borgon! Borgon, are you there?'

It was Grizzy and Mungoid and Hunjah.

Borgon slithered down the last slope, and they ran up to meet him.

'We got worried!' said Hunjah. 'The others are already back.'

'They said you were dead,' said Grizzy.

'Maybe I would have been, if it wasn't for my new friend,' said Borgon.

He opened the bag and the little yellow head popped up.

'Quammy!' said the duck.

'Cool!' said the others, and they gave her a stroke.

'So what happened?' asked Mungoid.

'The Raggahoos cheated,' said Borgon. 'So I'm going to teach them a lesson.'

Borgon pulled his axe from his belt.

'Hooray!' cheered Mungoid and Hunjah,

but Grizzy pulled a face.

'Don't do anything stupid,' she said.

'This is NOT stupid,' said Borgon. 'But it could be nasty, so hold my duck.'

He held the bag out towards Grizzy, but she refused to take it.

'It IS stupid!' she said. 'You can't just run up and attack the Raggahoos.'

'Why not?' demanded Borgon.

'The dame won't let you. And besides, everybody will just think you're being a bad loser for not getting up the mountain.'

'But I DID get up the mountain, and I can prove it!' said Borgon.

'It won't be easy,' said Grizzy.

'The Raggahoos will all say you're lying.'

'They wouldn't dare!' said Borgon, waving his axe. 'I'm a BARBARIAN!'

'Well, just for once, try to be a sensible barbarian,' said Grizzy. 'If the Raggahoos think you're dead, you can catch them by surprise. Hunjah, lend Borgon your hat.'

'What for?' asked Hunjah.

'You'll see!' said Grizzy.

What Do Lies Smell Like?

The four Raggahoos were on the stage, holding up the rubies and looking very pleased with themselves.

'I hereby declare that these four contenders have completed the first trial!' announced Madreesh.

'No they didn't!' shouted Grizzy from the

crowd. 'Three of them never went to the top of the mountain.'

The Raggahoos hissed angrily.

'But they have the rubies,' said the dame.

'I know,' said Grizzy. 'But ask them where they found the rubies. What were they in?'

'I can tell you that,' said Akabbah.

'Don't ask him,' said Grizzy. 'Ask the other three.'

The dame stared suspiciously at the fat one, the bony one and the one with curly hair.

'Well?' she said. 'Tell me. What were the rubies in?'

'Um . . . er . . . ah . . . well . . .' said the other three. But then their eyes opened wide in amazement. They were looking over the dame's shoulder.

Akabbah was standing behind her, flapping his arms, trying to give them a clue.

'A vulture?' said the bony one.

'Ha ha ha!' laughed the crowd.

Akabbah shook his head. He then pretended to pick up some twigs with his mouth and make a bird's nest.

'It's a cow eating grass,' said the one with curly hair.

The dame was so astonished by the answers that she hadn't looked round and seen what Akabbah was up to.

In desperation, Akabbah tried to pretend to be a bird laying an egg. He crouched down, and made it look as if he was pushing something big out.

'Wah ha ha ha ha!' screamed the crowd.

At last the dame looked round.

'What ARE you doing?' she demanded.

'He's trying to tell them it was a bird's
nest,' said Grizzy.

The dame called the Bigfoot to join her

on the stage.

'Did you put the rubies in a bird's nest?' she asked him.

The Bigfoot nodded. Madreesh looked down at Grizzy.

'How did you know that?' she asked.

'Borgon told me,' said Grizzy.

'But he's dead!' sneered Akabbah.

'You wish!' said Grizzy.

Then a chubby savage pushed his way on stage with a huge hat pulled down over his head.

'Who's that?' demanded Akabbah.

Borgon pulled the hat off.

'Gasp!' went the Raggahoos.

'Hooray!' cheered the crowd.

'So you finally got here, did you?' said
Akabbah, trying to stay calm. 'Well, you're
last, so you're eliminated.'

'At least I went to the top and back,' said
Borgon.

'Prove it!' sneered Akabbah. 'Where's your ruby?'

The dame turned to Borgon. 'I'm sorry, barbarian,' she said. 'You have to have a ruby to show you finished the trail.'

'Akabbah took all the rubies and gave them to his mates,' said Borgon. 'But he left behind a yellow egg. Look!'

Borgon reached into the bag and pulled out the pieces of eggshell.

'That's not an egg!' said Akabbah.

'No, but it WAS an egg,' said Borgon. 'And if you don't believe me, ask her.'

The little duck stuck her head out of the bag.

'Quammy!' she said.

The dame turned to the Bigfoot, who was nodding.

'So you DID go there!' said the dame.

'So did we!' shouted the other Raggahoos.

The dame stared at the three savages. Her long nose twitched suspiciously.

'Did you know that when there is a lie in

the air I can smell it?' she said. 'And we have
a severe punishment for lying!'

The blue slaves all came
up on to the stage and waved
their big heavy clubs with spikes
on them. The three cheating
Raggahoos shook with fear.

'DEATH DEATH DEATH!' cheered
the crowd.

'Er . . . no,' said the dame.

'HURT A LOT, HURT A LOT, HURT A
LOT!' chanted the crowd hopefully.

The dame shook her head.

'SLIGHLY SORE, SLIGHTLY SORE,
SLIGHTLY SORE!' chanted the crowd.

'NO!' said the dame. 'You will all be disqualified.'

'Booo!' went the crowd.

'Oh, thank you!' said the three Raggahoos, and they quickly got off the stage before the dame changed her mind.

'So I win, then!' said Akabbah. 'I'm the only one left.'

'No way!' shouted Grizzy. 'Borgon went up the mountain too! That's what this trial was all about, wasn't it?'

'The girl is right,' said Madreesh. 'The axeboy is still in the competition, so now prepare yourselves to face the next trial.'

A slave came over with two small shields

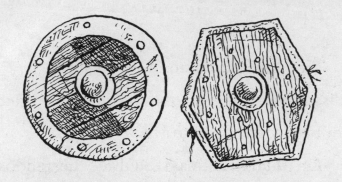

and passed one each to Borgon and Akabbah.

'Two little shields?' shouted Eyepatch Woman. 'Is that all they get?'

'Boring!' shouted Mr Rusty Teeth.

'Give them swords!' shouted Spike-Head Man.

'SWORDS!' echoed the crowd.

'No,' said Madreesh.

'What about daggers, then?' shouted Eyepatch Woman.

'DAGGERS?' shouted the crowd hopefully.

'No,' said Madreesh.

'Just give them anything dangerous,' cried out Mr Rusty Teeth.

'ANYTHING DANGEROUS!' cheered the crowd.

'No,' said Madreesh. 'This is the trial of a thousand darts.'

'The *what?*' said the crowd.

'You all get to throw darts at these two,' explained Madreesh. 'One thousand of them.'

'Hooray!' cheered everyone.

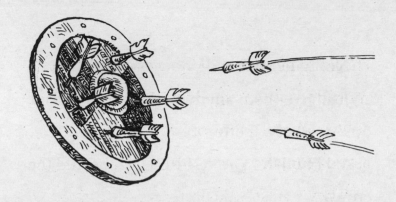

The Trial of a Thousand Darts

Borgon passed the picnic bag down to
Hunjah to keep the duck safe, then the blue
slaves wandered through the crowd handing
out little wooden darts.

'What's the point of this trial?' asked
Hunjah.

'It's to test their speed,' said Grizzy,

checking her book. 'Whoever catches the most darts on his shield wins.'

'But what if I hit Borgon by accident?' asked Hunjah.

'They're just little darts,' said Mungoid. 'They won't hurt much.'

'It doesn't matter about hurting,' said Grizzy. 'If either of them get hit, they get disqualified.'

'I don't want to risk it,' said Hunjah. 'I'm going to have my lunch instead.' He reached into his tunic and pulled out a string of tomatoes. 'Do you want one, Mungoid?'

'Yuk, no thanks!' said the chunky savage.
He was clutching a pile of darts all ready
to throw.

The rest of the crowd were buzzing with
excitement, and some of them were getting
out their daggers and spears to throw as well.

'I'm watching you all,' warned Madreesh.
'When the trumpet sounds, you just throw
the darts. You do NOT throw anything else!'

'Aw!' moaned the crowd.

Madreesh got off the stage, just leaving
Borgon and Akabbah holding their little
shields.

The fat blue slave took a deep breath and
gave his trumpet a mighty blow.

TUB-OW!

A little dart had flown out of the crowd and stuck itself into his nose.

'Ha ha ha!' went everybody.

The slave tugged out the dart and looked a bit grumpy.

'Blow it again,' said Madreesh.

'I'm not in the mood now,' said the slave.

'PLEASE!' begged the crowd.

'I'm not blowing my trumpet until you say sorry,' said the slave.

'SORRY!' cheered the crowd.

'Oh all right, then,' said the slave.

TUB-ARP!

A shower of darts flew at the stage.

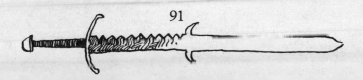

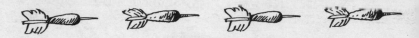

Borgon's first reaction was to duck, but Akabbah dived straight at them, skipping his long legs in the air and waving his shield around.

THUPPA PLUPPA DONK!

Akabbah's shield was already filling up with darts, so Borgon had to catch up quickly. He ran around, holding out his shield and trying not to be hit. More darts came whistling through the air, some landing on the floor, some flying off to the side, and a few just skimming past his hair and clothes.

Borgon thought he was doing rather well, until he saw Akabbah's shield was already completely full.

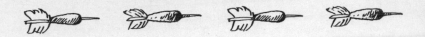

'You're too slow, barbarian!' said the tall savage mockingly. 'It's all over and I've got lots more than you.'

'Hey, Borgon, over here!' shouted Mungoid. He had kept a whole handful of darts back, and he threw them all at once.

'Thanks!' cried Borgon, reaching out to catch them. Akabbah was behind him and couldn't get there first, so instead he gave

Borgon a shove in the back and sent the barbarian flying forwards. Borgon landed flat on his tummy, but he just managed to stretch up his arm.

THIBBA DOBBA!

Mungoid's darts buried themselves on the very edge of the shield.

'There!' said Borgon proudly. 'We've both got a shield full. So what happens now?'

'This!' said Akabbah.

A single dart came slicing through the air, and hit Borgon right on the bottom.

'**YEE-OW!**' yelped Borgon.

RAGGA RAGGA HOO HOO! came a shout from the crowd. The savage with the

curly hair was holding a small crossbow and
looked very pleased with himself.

'Good shot!' said Akabbah. 'Borgon got
hit, so he is disqualified. I win!'

'I will decide who wins,' said Madreesh as

she got back on to the stage.

'It has to be me,' said Akabbah. 'I never got hit.'

'But that last dart was cheating!' shouted Mungoid.

'No it wasn't,' said Akabbah. 'It was a clever plan, and Borgon should have been ready for it. After all, if you want to be the Prince's Shadow, you should be ready for anything. Well, am I right?'

Madreesh nodded sadly. 'I suppose so,' she said.

Down in the crowd, Hunjah was looking gloomy.

'I can't believe Borgon lost because of

that,' he said. 'It's put me right off my lunch.'

'Can I have your last tomato, then?' asked Grizzy.

'Are you sure?' said Hunjah. 'It's a bit green and mouldy.'

'That's exactly how I like them!' grinned Grizzy.

Up on the stage Akabbah was still strutting around proudly.

'I'd make the perfect Shadow!' he was saying. 'I'm always on my guard, expecting the unexpected. Nothing ever catches me out . . .'

SPLOTCH!

One green mouldy
tomato hit him
right in the teeth
and exploded
all over his face.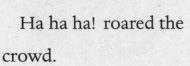

Ha ha ha! roared the
crowd.

'I call this trial a draw,' smiled Madreesh.
'So you will both face the third and final test.
Prepare for the Walk of Death!'

'Wooo!' went the crowd.

The Walk of Death

Everybody went to gather round a large
hole in the ground. The sides were steep and
smooth and a long rope was stretched tightly
across the middle. Grizzy, Mungoid and
Hunjah peered over the edge.

GURR-ARGHH!

A huge sabre-toothed bear was prowling
around the pit. It had toenails like bananas

and claws like daggers. The bottom of the
pit was littered with skulls and bones.

'Wow!' said Mungoid. 'She is a BEAUTY.'
The blue slaves had taken Borgon and

Akabbah to stand at opposite ends of the long rope. Grizzy, Hunjah and Mungoid made their way round to join Borgon, while the other Raggahoos went to support Akabbah.

Madreesh was standing on the very edge of the pit, leaning on her staff. She was just about to speak when the bear lunged up and tried to swipe a giant claw at her.

GURR-ARGHII!

'Behave yourself,' said Madreesh.

GURR-ARGHH!

'I said behave!' she said sharply. She thrust the end of her staff down at the bear, and waggled the silver crystal in front of the

snarling face. The great beast
tried to shy away, but as the
crystal twisted and flickered in the
sunlight the bear couldn't take its
eyes off it. Suddenly the dame flicked
the end of the staff upwards. The
beast fell over backwards and collapsed
on to a heap of old bones.

KERR-UNCH!

'Oh cool!' said Grizzy. 'I SO wish I
could do that.'

'Contestants, you will take turns to walk
across the rope,' announced Madreesh.
'Keep going until one of you gives up . . .'

'Boring!' shouted the crowd.

'. . . or falls in.'

'Hooray!' cheered the crowd.

By this time the bear was back on its feet and looking crosser than ever.

'You go first, little chubby guts,' called out Akabbah from across the pit. 'That bear looks ready for a good meal.'

'Why don't you go first?' shouted Mungoid.

'Can't he speak for himself?' said Akabbah. 'Or is he too scared?'

'SCARED?' cursed Borgon, clutching his axe. 'Nobody tells a barbarian he's scared.'

'I just did,' said Akabbah. 'So come over here and get me if you dare!'

Borgon hissed angrily, then held out his axe to balance himself. He stepped on to the rope with one foot, then very carefully he put his second foot on too. Below him the bear's blood-red eyes were looking up, his teeth and claws all ready.

'Good luck, Borgon!' shouted Mungoid. 'Dash over as fast as you can.'

'No!' shouted Hunjah. 'There's no rush. Go slow,

one step at a time.'

Borgon was already starting to wobble and the bear was licking its lips.

'How about you, Grizzy?' asked Borgon. 'What do you say?'

'Goodbye,' said Grizzy. 'It was nice knowing you.'

Borgon bit his lip and took a tiny step forwards. The bear stretched itself up and opened its mouth wide. The thick purple tongue lashed around hungrily, licking its long curved teeth. Over on the far side the Raggahoos were laughing.

Borgon felt the rope twitching. He looked

across to see Akabbah had his foot on the far
end and was bouncing it up and down.

'Get on with it!' shouted Akabbah. 'We
haven't got all day.'

'Why don't YOU try?' shouted Grizzy.

The crowd agreed. They all turned to point
at Akabbah.

'GO GO! GO!' they chanted.

Akabbah broke into a big laugh.

'Oh all right, if you insist.'

Akabbah ran forwards and launched himself straight off the edge. He landed neatly on the rope and sprinted all the way across to where Borgon was struggling to keep his balance. The lanky savage gave Borgon a sharp prod in the guts, dashed back

and then leapt off with a high backflip and landed perfectly on his feet. Down in the pit the bear lumbered around in confusion as the crowd erupted with noise.

RAGGA RAGGA HOO HOO!
RAGGA RAGGA HOO HOO!

Akabbah was grinning and bowing and lapping up the applause.

'Your turn!' he called over to Borgon.

Borgon was still on his end of the rope, trying to keep his balance.

'Barbarian, you have already

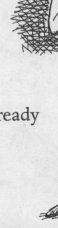

done well,' said Madreesh. 'You can give up now and still depart with honour.'

'And lose to HIM?' said Borgon. 'No way!'

And with that, he took a big step out over the pit.

'Ooooh!' went the crowd.

GURR-ARGHH! went the bear.

Borgon took another step, and then another . . . but then he stumbled! He threw himself forwards and dashed the rest of the way, almost knocking Akabbah over on the other side.

'It's easy,' gasped Borgon.

"Then back you go again,' said Akabbah, giving Borgon a hard push.

Borgon staggered backwards over the pit. Mungoid and Hunjah just managed to grab him before he fell and pulled him to safety.

'Fantastic!' said Mungoid. 'You can do it!'

Borgon took a few deep breaths to calm himself.

'So what happens now?' he said. 'Do we just keep going backwards and forwards all day?'

'You're right,' shouted Akabbah from the far side. 'Let's hurry it up!'

He skipped across to the middle of the rope, then bounced up and down to make it stretch.

CREAK PING TWANG!

The bear leapt up and just caught the rope with the tip of a claw. Akabbah had to wave his arms madly to keep his balance, then quickly ran back to his side of the pit.

'All ready for you!' he called over to Borgon.

Borgon stepped on to the rope.

'Just go very gently,' said Hunjah. 'He
was bouncing, but you should be fine if you
tiptoe along.'

'Tiptoe?' snapped Borgon. 'I'm a
BARBARIAN about to cross a BEAR PIT.
And you want me to tiptoe like a little
pixie?'

'It was just a thought,' said Hunjah.

Borgon stepped out over the pit. Last
time the rope had been almost level, but
this time it was sloping downwards and it
was wobbling more. The bear was waiting
with its teeth and claws ready. Borgon slid

his feet along the rope as carefully as he could.

Grizzy, Mungoid and Hunjah were so busy watching him, that they didn't notice the other three Raggahoos had pushed through the crowd behind them.

'Give me that!' said the fat one, snatching the bag from Hunjah.

'What do you want?' demanded Hunjah.

'We saw you eating those tomatoes,' said the one with curly hair. 'We're just making sure you haven't got any more to throw.'

'He didn't throw it,' said Grizzy. 'I did.'

'Oh really?' said the bony one. 'Then here's a present from Akabbah.'

He raised his fist, but Mungoid stepped in the way.

'If you want to hit somebody, try me,' he said.

'You asked for it!' said the bony one, and he punched Mungoid hard on the chin.

WUMCH!

'Yow!' squealed the bony one.

He staggered back, clutching his fingers. Mungoid hadn't even blinked.

'Feel better for that?' smiled the chunky savage. 'It must be my turn now. Line yourselves up!'

But the three Raggahoos didn't wait. They dashed away, dropping the bag on the ground. Something small and yellow rolled out, but at that moment there was a noise from across the pit . . .

TWING!

They all looked to see Borgon had reached the middle of the rope. A tiny strand had snapped under his feet.

Borgon took another step.

PLINK TWOING!

Borgon smiled to himself. The rope wasn't going to last much longer. All he had to do was get across and back, then surely the silly prancing savage would end up in the pit!

'Quammy!'

What?

'Quammy! Quammy!'

'Come back!' shouted Grizzy.

Borgon looked round and saw the little duck was toddling down the rope to join him.

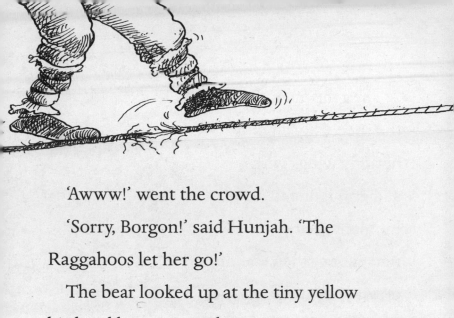

'Awww!' went the crowd.

'Sorry, Borgon!' said Hunjah. 'The Raggahoos let her go!'

The bear looked up at the tiny yellow bird and let out a mighty roar.

GURR-ARGHHHH!

The duck started to wobble. She stumbled about, first on one leg and then the other.

'Ooooh!' said the crowd.

Then the duck slipped off
the rope. She flapped
her tiny wings with
all her might and for a
moment she hovered in
mid-air, but then she drifted
down and hit the bottom of the
pit with a sad little **THUD**.

'**ARGHHH!**' screamed the crowd.

The bear lunged towards the duck
with its claws raised.

'Oh no you DON'T!' cried Borgon.

The bear looked up and saw the chubby
little savage glaring down and waving his
axe.

'I'm warning you,' said Borgon. 'Get back from that duck.'

The bear ignored him and went for the little yellow bird. There was only one thing a proper barbarian could do.

'YARGHHHH!'

With a loud scream, the axeboy leapt off the rope and hurled himself into the pit.

Two Against One

WHAM BASH CHOP GRUNT!

Borgon's axe flashed, his feet kicked and
his teeth chomped. He had attacked so fast
that the giant bear had no idea what had hit
it. It backed away a couple of steps, then
looked down at the chubby little savage.

'So you thought you'd attack my duck, did

you?' snarled Borgon. 'I'm going to have to teach you a lesson.'

'Quammy,' said the little duck, and she waved her wing in a menacing way.

'You'd better keep out of it,' said Borgon to the duck. 'Two against one isn't fair.'

The crowd were starting to laugh.

'Come on, bear!' shouted Akabbah, looking over the edge. 'Finish him off, then I can be the winner.'

The bear lurched forwards and swiped its giant paw round to scoop Borgon's head off, but the paw passed clean through empty air. Borgon had already ducked, but then he suddenly leapt up and smacked his axe hard into the bear's long teeth.

KRINTCH!

The bear howled and lashed out, knocking Borgon flying into the wall. The barbarian ended up lying face down in a pile of old bones without moving.

'Ooooh!' cheered the crowd.

'GET UP, BORGON!' shouted Mungoid and Hunjah.

'THIS IS NO TIME FOR A SLEEP!' shouted Grizzy.

Borgon was too dazed to hear them, but then he felt a peck on his ear.

'Quammy quammy quammy!' squeaked the little duck.

'What?' said Borgon. He opened his eyes just in time to see the great bear launch itself at him. He rolled to the side.

WHUMPAH!

The bear hit the ground with a mighty, lung-bruising bellyflop.

'Quammy!' said the duck excitedly.

'Thanks for the warning, little friend!' said Borgon.

As the gasping bear slowly pulled itself to its feet, Borgon ran round it in circles, taking swipes with his axe. The bear twisted and turned, swinging its paws wildly, trying to fend him off but the barbarian was too fast. Eventually the beast staggered off to the side of the pit and sat down. Its teeth were smarting, it was covered in nasty scratches, its ribs ached and it was out of breath. It had had enough.

'What's your problem?' screamed Borgon. 'I've seen little ducks that are braver than you. Now, come on, let's finish this off.'

He raised his axe, took a deep breath and got ready to charge.

'**YARGHHHHHH . . .**'
PLANG!

Borgon found himself tangled up in a steel net. His arms were trapped and his feet wouldn't move. The only thing he could do was fall over, so that's what he did.

'BOOO!' went the crowd.

'What's going on?' demanded Borgon, looking upwards.

The two slaves who had thrown the net stepped aside. Madreesh looked over the edge of the pit.

'We had to stop you somehow,' smiled the dame. 'The bear's supposed to attack YOU, not the other way round!'

Small, Fat and Far Too Smelly

TUB-ARP went the fat blue slave on his double-headed trumpet. He hadn't done a good tub-arp for a while and was getting a bit bored. Madreesh was back on the stage, standing between Borgon and Akabbah.

'It is time for me to decide who is to be the Prince's new Shadow,' said the dame.

'I was the first back from the mountain,'

said Akabbah. 'And I never fell off the rope, so the rules say I win!'

'I know what the rules say,' said the dame crossly. 'It was me who made them up!'

'Forget the rules!' shouted Grizzy from the crowd. 'If you want a bodyguard for the prince, you haven't tested the most important thing.'

'What's that?' asked Madreesh.

'Loyalty!' said Grizzy. 'Borgon would risk his life for the prince.'

'How do you know that?' demanded Akabbah.

'Because that's what he does,' said Grizzy. 'He even risked his life for a duck!'

'That's true,' said Madreesh. 'He has also shown exceptional strength and courage.'

'But he's mad!' shouted Akabbah. 'The prince needs somebody calm and reliable. That fat kid is totally out of control.'

Borgon's hand immediately went to his axe, but before he could pull it from his belt, Grizzy hissed at him.

'Ignore him, Borgon!' she said. 'Don't ruin it now. You could win this!'

Borgon looked back at Akabbah and smiled sweetly.

Akabbah pushed past Madreesh and shoved his nose right into Borgon's face.

'You can't be the Prince's Shadow.

You're too small, you're too fat and you're
FAR too smelly.'

Borgon's knuckles were going white, but
still his axe remained tucked safely in his belt.

'Well?' said Akabbah. 'Are you just going
to stand there and let anybody say what they
like to you? What kind of savage are you?'

'Small, fat, smelly, mad and totally out of
control,' said Borgon.

'There!' said Akabbah to everyone. 'He said it himself. Are you really going to let him win?'

Madreesh examined Borgon carefully. His hand had relaxed on his axe, he was breathing calmly, he even had a smile on his face. Down in the crowd, Mungoid and Hunjah started to chant:

'Borgon, Borgon, Borgon . . .'

Quickly it caught on. The noise got louder

and louder as everyone joined in:

BORGON! BORGON! BORGON!

The dame needed to be certain. She looked over to the blue slaves. They were all just scratching their noses like they didn't care, but secretly they were pointing their fingers at Borgon.

'Well done, barbarian,' said Madreesh. 'Not only have you faced the other challenges, you have just overcome the

hardest challenge of all. You have proved
your self-control. Therefore it gives me great
pleasure to announce . . .'

'NO!' shrieked Akabbah. 'I can't believe
it! The only reason you've picked him is
because he made friends with that stupid,
horrible, ugly little duck.'

'What did you say?' said Borgon.

'Ignore him!' said Grizzy.

'WHAT DID YOU SAY?' roared Borgon,
marching up to Akabbah.

The tall boy took a nervous step
backwards.

'See? See?' whimpered Akabbah. 'He's
mad!'

'I know I'm mad,' said Borgon. 'And small and fat and smelly. You can say what you like about me, it's all true. BUT NOBODY INSULTS MY DUCK.'

He launched himself at Akabbah. The tall boy tried to skip aside, but Borgon was too fast. He caught Akabbah's ankle with the edge of his axe and sent him sprawling across the stage. Akabbah tried to pull his sword, but Borgon charged forwards and kicked the blade out of his hand. Akabbah was lying on his back, with the axeboy standing on his chest, axe raised high in the air.

'Say SORRY!' ordered Borgon.

'I'm sorry, Borgon!' whimpered Akabbah.

'No!' said Borgon. 'You've got to say sorry to the DUCK.'

'The duck?' repeated Akabbah. 'I'm not saying sorry to a duck! How mad are you?'

'You're about to find out!' screamed Borgon.

Suddenly Borgon was dazzled by a flash of white light. Something was flickering in his face and all he could do was stare as it made pretty swoops and circles in the air. Borgon's head went up and down and twisted and turned, and his whole body started to feel heavy. He staggered away from Akabbah

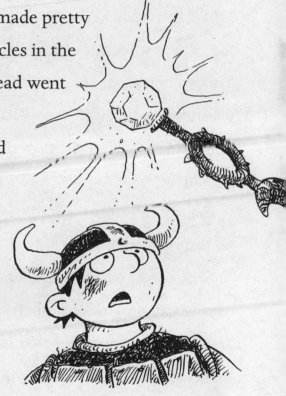

and the next thing he knew there was a loud clatter. Pain shot from his foot.

'Yow!' yelped Borgon.

He realised he'd dropped his axe on his toe. It was sore, but at least he wasn't being dazzled any more. He saw that Madreesh was holding her staff away from him, releasing him from the power of the silver crystal.

'Are you all right?' asked the dame.

Borgon nodded.

'Sorry about that,' she said. 'But I could see it was going to get messy, and some of us aren't really dressed for that sort of thing.'

Akabbah was back on his feet. He stomped

up to Madreesh.

'See?' said Akabbah. 'There's no way he can be the winner now!'

The dame slipped the end of her staff between his feet and gave it a sharp flick. Akabbah's legs flew out from under him. He tumbled off the edge of the stage and crashed down on to the stony ground.

WHUMP!

The laughs from the crowd were enough to tell him that it was time to give up.

'And so, Borgon,' said the dame, 'as I was about to say, it gives me great pleasure to announce that you are . . . THE PRINCE'S SHADOW!'

'Hooray!' cheered the crowd.

TUB-ARP! went the double-headed trumpet.

But Borgon shook his head.

'No thanks,' he said. 'Goodbye.'

Then he jumped off the stage to join his friends.

'Ha ha ha!' they all laughed. 'Good one, Borgon!'

Madreesh was astonished.

'No, wait!' she called out, then she hurried down the steps to join them. 'If you never wanted to be the Shadow, why did you put yourself through the trials?'

'Those Raggahoos were getting on my nerves,' said Borgon.

'He wanted to teach them a lesson,' explained Grizzy.

'He won, they lost, job done,' grinned Mungoid.

'Can you seriously imagine Borgon being at the palace with all you posh types?' asked Hunjah.

'He'll get a really smart uniform,' said Madreesh.

'Borgon in a uniform?' giggled Grizzy.

'Of course!' said Madreesh. 'The Shadow dresses up so he can go wherever the prince goes.'

'All the time?' asked Hunjah.

'Oh yes,' said Madreesh. 'Even when he's at the perfume baths.'

'PERFUME BATHS!' they all laughed.

'I've never had a bath in my life,' said Borgon. 'Yuk!'

The crowd were all starting to drift off, and a few of them were saying 'well done!' and patting Borgon on the back as they passed.

'I wish you'd think about it,' said Madreesh. 'We really need you.'

'I know what might change his mind,' said Mungoid. 'Would Borgon get to eat whatever the prince eats?'

'Of course,' said Madreesh. 'Everybody at the palace eats the same as the prince. You can have as much as you like.'

'I like the sound of that!' said Borgon. 'I hope he likes elephant tongues and hippo steaks.'

'Er . . . actually the prince has a very special diet,' said the dame. 'It's mainly nuts and roots, with a little bit of sour cream as a treat.'

'Ha ha ha!' they all laughed again.

'Honestly!' said Borgon. 'Uniforms,

baths, nuts and roots . . . who'd want a job
like that?'

Grizzy pointed at a sad
figure sitting all alone on
the ground. Akabbah
was still where he'd
landed.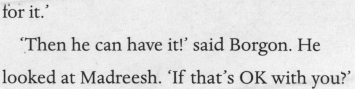

'Him,' she said.
'He was prepared
to do anything
for it.'

'Then he can have it!' said Borgon. He
looked at Madreesh. 'If that's OK with you?'

'I suppose he was the best of the rest,'
said the dame. 'But you were the winner.

You deserve to get something.'

'Really?' said Borgon. He thought for a moment. 'Then perhaps you could do me a favour?'

The Night Visitor

'Hey, Dad! Mum! Guess what? I WON I WON
I WON!'

Borgon ran into the cave to find nothing
had changed since the morning. It was just as
he expected. His mum was still trying to pull
her hair straight with her fingers, and his dad
still had only one sock.

'You won what?' asked Fulgut. He was in the middle of swapping his sock over so that his cold foot could have a turn at being warm.

'The Shadow Trials!' said Borgon proudly.

'I thought you were only going to watch,' said Fulma.

'I was, but those Raggahoos were so smug, I had to take them on,' said Borgon. 'And I won!'

Fulma gave Fulgut a poke in the ribs.

'You said they'd never let a barbarian into the palace!' she said. 'So, Borgon, when do you start being the Shadow?'

'Er . . . well, I don't,' said Borgon. 'They've given the job to a Raggahoo.'

'Sec?' blasted Fulgut. 'I TOLD YOU! Those palace types are all cheats and liars.'

'They didn't cheat,' said Borgon. 'They were pretty fair actually.'

'Oh really?' said Fulgut. 'You might think they were being fair, but that's how good they are at cheating. You don't even know you've been cheated!'

'I was NOT cheated!' said Borgon.

'Oh yes you were,' said Fulgut.

'NOT!' shouted Borgon.

'WERE!' shouted Fulgut.

Fulma sighed.

'Stop it, you two!' she said. 'Let's have tea.'

'Good idea!' said Borgon. 'So long as it

isn't nuts and roots.'

'Nuts and roots?' gasped Fulgut.

'It's camel-hump pie,' said Fulma.

She put a large dish on the table with a huge lumpy pie in it.

'YUM!' said Borgon.

Just then a horse galloped up to the cave

pulling a silver chariot.

'It looks like somebody from the palace,' said Fulma.

'It's the dame!' said Borgon. 'Perfect timing.'

Madreesh let go of the reins and stepped down from the chariot.

'May I come in?' she asked.

'What do you want?' snapped Fulgut suspiciously.

'Borgon was our winner today,' said Madreesh. 'So I've brought some special prizes.'

'He doesn't want them,' snapped Fulgut. 'Now go away.'

'They're not for him, they're for you,' said Madreesh.

She handed over two boxes, one to Fulgut and one to Fulma. Fulma opened hers first.

'Oooh!' she said in an excited, squeaky voice. 'Is this really for me?'

Madreesh nodded.

Fulma took out a long silver comb with two hundred teeth, then hurried over to her mirror. Even before the comb touched it, her hair was starting to straighten out and behave itself.

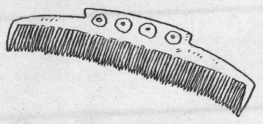

'It's wonderful!' she said. 'Thank you.'

Everybody stared at Fulgut.

'Open it, dear,' said Fulma.

'There's nothing I want from the palace!' said Fulgut.

'Oh yes there is,' grinned Borgon.

Fulgut ripped open the box. A huge smile crossed his face.

'That's just perfect!' he said.

He pulled out a thick blue sock and put it on his bare foot. For a moment he smiled happily but then he suddenly turned on Madreesh.

'HANG ON!' he said. 'You're trying to

bribe us, to make up for Borgon not being the Prince's Shadow. You posh palace types don't like common barbarians do you? We're NOT GOOD ENOUGH for you, are we?'

The big old barbarian stamped his feet in fury. It would have been better if he'd been wearing his big boots to make some loud **CRUNCH WAM BASH!** noises, but his blue socks just went **PIFF POFF PUFF!** It sounded a bit feeble, but Madreesh had the good manners not to laugh.

'I asked Borgon to come to the palace, but he refused,' said Madreesh.

'Is that right, Borgon?' asked Fulma.

Borgon nodded.

'Why would he do that?' demanded
Fulgut.

Madreesh was staring at the pie.

'Your camel-hump pie might have
something to do with it,' she said. Her long
nose was twitching hungrily. 'We never get
anything like that at the palace.'

'They only get to eat nuts and roots,' said
Borgon. 'And they have perfume
baths.'

'What?' gasped Fulgut. 'That's disgusting!
I wouldn't let my son go to that palace if
you begged me.'

'There you are, Fulgut!' laughed Fulma.
'You said the palace wouldn't let Borgon

in, but it turns out it's you who wouldn't let him go!'

'Yes, well . . . maybe that's true,' said Fulgut sheepishly. He looked down at his new sock and wiggled his toes. 'Sorry if I was a bit rude,' he said to the dame.

'That's quite all right,' sighed Madreesh. She was still looking at the pie. 'Well, I'd better be going. I've got my nuts and roots waiting for me.'

'Hang on,' said Fulgut.

He quickly took a great spoon and scooped a huge dollop of pie on to a palm leaf. He held it out towards the dame.

'I can't,' said Madreesh. 'I'm not allowed to.'

'Go on,' said Fulma. 'Take it.'

The dame's nose took a deep sniff.

'Scorpion gravy!' she gasped. 'I haven't had that in years.'

'Then ride back slowly,' grinned Borgon. 'You can eat it on the way.'

'We won't tell if you don't!' laughed Fulgut.

Madreesh quickly took the pie, then stepped back up on to her chariot.

'Thank you,' she said. 'And especially thank you, Borgon. It was the best Shadow Trials we've ever had!'

The dame gave her horse a slap on the

bottom, then with a smile and a wave she
was gone.

Fulma looked at Borgon with a puzzled
expression on her face.

'I don't understand,' she said. 'You won the
competition, so why did you ask her to bring

these things for us?'

'Because when you wake up tomorrow, you'll have a comb and Dad will have his other sock,' said Borgon.

'So what?' said Fulma.

'So then you can stop worrying about the stupid things, and you can concentrate on being proper barbarians again!' said Borgon.

'Ho ho ho!' laughed Fulgut. 'You're right, son. And I'm very proud of you.'

'I still think it's a shame that you didn't get a prize for yourself,' said Fulma.

'Oh I got the best prize of all,' said Borgon.

He opened his bag and a little head
popped out.

'Quammy!'

Who's the Mummy?

As the evening fire died down to a warm red glow, the little duck toddled round the cave to check on everybody. The big old savage was snoring away with his feet warmly wrapped in his socks. The lady had dozed off by the mirror having tried out twenty new hairstyles, and the small chubby barbarian was stuffed full of pie and lying fast asleep by the fire.

The little duck needed to sleep too. She had started the day inside an egg, then ran round the mountains, then helped to fight a giant bear and finally she'd had some scorpion gravy for tea. Not many little ducks have a first day like that, so no wonder she was tired!

She knew that she should be looking for a nest and a mummy duck, but it didn't matter because she knew where she would be warm and safe. She toddled over to where her new friend was lying. As softly as she could, she climbed up on to Borgon's head and nestled down in his hair.

'Quammy,' she said happily, then she
closed her eyes and went to sleep.